This book belongs to:

Magic Wand

Other books in the series:

Best Friends

Magic Sprinkles

Tea Party

Copyright © 2011 make believe ideas ltd.
The Wilderness, Berkhamsted, Hertfordshire, HP4 2AZ, UK.
565 Royal Parkway, Nashville, TN 37214, USA.

Reading together

This book is designed to be fun for children who are just starting to read on their own. They will enjoy and benefit from some time discussing the story with an adult. Encourage them to pause and talk about what is happening in the pictures. Help them to spot familiar words and sound out the letters in harder words. Look at the following ways you can help your child take those first steps in reading:

Look at rhymes

The sentences in this book are written with simple rhymes. Encourage your child to recognize the rhyming words. Try asking the following questions:

- What does this word say?

- Can you find a word that rhymes with it?

- Look at the ending of two rhyming words, are they spelled the same? For example, "grand" and "hand."

Test understanding

It is one thing to understand one word at a time, but it is important to make sure your child can understand the story as a whole!

Ask your child questions as you read the story, for example:

- Do you like Camilla's wand?

- Did Camilla buy a new wand?

- Which wand did Camilla like best?

- Play "find the obvious mistake." Read the text as your child looks at the words with you, but make an obvious mistake to see if he or she catches it. Ask your child to correct you and provide the right word.

Activity section

A "Ready to tell" section at the end of the book encourages children to remember what happened in the story and then retell it. A dictionary page helps children to increase their vocabulary, and a useful word page reinforces their knowledge of the most common words. There is also a practical activity inspired by the story and a "Camilla and her friends" section where children can learn about all of Camilla the Cupcake Fairy's friends!

5

Camilla was in town one day
when something caught her eye,

a window full of shiny wands
for fairy folks to buy!

Wanderful

Wanderful

8

Camilla loved her wand,
but just like hats and shoes,
you can never have
too many wands,
so which one would she choose?

First she saw a tall one,
that felt elegant and grand.

Then she held a tiny one
that fell right through her hand!

Next she saw a sparkly one,
covered in jewels and hearts.

Then she saw
an odd-shaped one,
made from old spare parts!

Gold and pink and purple,
Camilla loved them all.
But though they were all special,
one wand was best of all . . .

The one wand that she really loved,
the wand that felt just right,
was the one that she'd had all along,
and she squeezed its handle tight!

Ready to tell

Can you remember what happened in the story? Look at each picture and then try retelling the story.

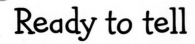

23

Camilla's fairy dictionary

choose When you choose something, you pick it from a group.

wand A wand is a stick that fairies use to make magical things happen.

grand When something is grand, it is amazing in its size or the way it looks.

jewel A jewel is a stone that is shiny and sometimes brightly colored. Jewels can cost a lot of money to buy.

squeeze To squeeze something is to hold or hug it very tightly.

sparkly When something is sparkly, it shines and glitters.

Camilla's useful words

Here are some key words used in context. Make simple sentences for the other words in the border.

Camilla was **in** town one day.

She went shopping for a new wand.

Camilla tried a tall one **and** a small one.

Camilla tried **a** wand that sparkled.

She liked **her** wand best of all.

Camilla and her friends

Camilla loves making cupcakes and using her wand to make magical toppings! She sometimes gets a little confused, but she never gives up and is a true friend to the other cupcake fairies.

Connie loves art and crafts. She's always drawing, painting, or gluing. Most of all, she loves making gifts for her friends.

Molly is kind, thoughtful, and a bit of a dreamer. She's always coming up with new things to do and try. Sometimes they are a little crazy!

Maya is super-smart. She's always reading recipe books and inventing new cakes and toppings. Her favorite day of the year is Cupcake Day when all the fairies have a bake-off!

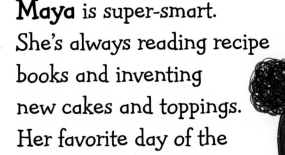

Carrie is full of energy, and she is always on the go! She loves rushing around on her roller skates and is crazy about all sports, especially soccer.

Sally Swish runs the Wanderful wand shop. She sells every kind of wand you can imagine!

Cranberry is Camilla's cat. He's a little lazy but loves to join in Camilla's adventures — especially if they involve cupcakes, which they usually do!

Miss Sprinkles

is the cupcake fairies'
teacher. She is very kind and wise and will
always help the fairies if they have a problem.

Sandy Swirls has a very

important job: delivering the
fairy mail! On a cupcake fairy's
fifth birthday, Sandy
delivers their very
first magic wand.

Make a fairy wand!

You will need:

2 sheets of yellow paper
scissors
a stick or an old pen or pencil
sticky tape
glue
1 sheet of pink paper
marker pens
silver glitter
ribbon

Camilla loves her magic wand. Make a wand of your very own!

What to do:

1. Put the two pieces of yellow paper together, one on top of the other. Draw a big star on one of them and then ask a grown-up to cut around it. Make sure they are cutting two pieces of paper! This should give you two stars that look exactly the same.

2. Next, lay the top of your stick over one of the stars. Attach it to the star with a piece of tape and put drops of glue around it. Lay your second star over the top and press it down so that they stick together.

3. To make the jewels for the center of your wand, draw two hearts on the pink piece of paper and ask a grown-up to help cut them out. Glue a heart to the center of the star on both sides of the wand.

4. For a finishing touch, put dots of glue around the star and sprinkle with glitter, or make gems out of pieces of silver foil.

5. Finally, tie a ribbon to the handle with a big bow. Now your wand looks just like Camilla's!

For an extra-special wand:

- Decorate your wand with sparkly candy wrappers or real gem stickers.

- Use ribbons to decorate your wand handle.